WHAT PARENTS ARE SAYING ABOUT THE IMAGINE SERIES

"I felt the author did a great job pulling the reader into the story. I felt like I was actually in the story."

–Patti Pierce, author of
Truth and Grace Homeschool Academy blog

". . .a fun read which kept us turning pages, imagining what it may have been like during Noah's time and remembering that things change, but God doesn't, and we should always be thankful. I would definitely recommend the story to those looking for clean reading for kids and biblical fiction!"

–Martianne Stanger, author of *Training Happy Hearts* blog

"This one is a page-turner. Once you start, you won't want to put it down. The writing fills your imagination with vivid imagery. One thing that was fun for us to discuss, after everyone had a turn with the book, was how the [story] aligned with the Bible."

–Crystal Heft, author of *Living Abundantly* blog

". . .a great book and we loved reading it aloud together! I recommend you grabbing a copy for your own family to read!"

–Felicia Mollohan, author o̶f̶ ̶.̶.̶.̶ *Life* blog

IMAGINE
THE FALL OF JERICHO

Matt
Koceich

BARBOUR BOOKS
An Imprint of Barbour Publishing, Inc.

Member of the
Evangelical Christian
Publishers Association

THOUSANDS OF YEARS AGO

The walls exploded. Rocks shot past him in all directions. Groaning from somewhere deep within the ground beneath his feet threatened an even worse fate than being pulverized by the collapsing city. The race had finally come to an end. Despite all his hard work and standing up to a very wicked man, the falling city of Jericho was seconds away from ending all of the boy's hard work.

Just an hour before, twelve-year-old Jake Henry had been racing through the gigantic maze of stone houses and secret passages. He had fought bravely against the evil Ka'nah but didn't have the power to stand up against the forces of nature that were churning around him now. He managed a final burst of speed, but before he could jump out over a chasm where a house used to be, the ground disappeared from under his feet. He fell backward, down into the darkness of the broken earth.

As he fell, Jake looked up and saw Ka'nah looking out over the chasm. The evil one jumped and kept the sword out in front of his body. Jake could only guess that the villain was laughing.

Jake crashed onto a pile of jagged stones. It was like diving backward into a concrete ocean. Stars of pain and light shot over the backs of his eyelids. Fire shot through his arms and legs. It felt like some invisible monster hand had squeezed his body and busted every bone. Twice. All of these sensations mixed together and brought Jake a great deal of pain. The hurt washed over him like a tidal wave and carried him away from consciousness.

ooooo

Muted sounds of voices came to Jake through the rubble. The sounds of men seeking their prey. Angry and determined tones grew louder and clearer.

"Here's another one!"

But that didn't matter now, because Ka'nah was right above Jake, blade extended, zooming down on him.

Jake shut his eyes and screamed.

CHAPTER 1

PRESENT DAY

NORTH CAROLINA
3:33 P.M.

Jake stared out the side window of his parents' minivan. The Appalachian Mountains passed in a blur of hurried green streaks. He was supposed to be headed to camp with Danny, but that fell through when Danny's mom called saying that her only son had a 101 fever and wouldn't be going anywhere. Jake figured, incorrectly, that Danny's illness would translate into a SKIP CAMP pass for himself. No such luck. Here he was getting shuttled across northwest North Carolina to attend Oak Bay Camp. With no buddy. For a whole week. Joy.

"You should work on having a positive attitude," Jake's dad said from behind the steering wheel. "When I was your age, I would have given a lot of money to be able to go to summer camp."

Jake bit his tongue. He wanted to tell his father that he'd be more than happy to trade places. But he didn't want to be disrespectful. He knew his parents paid big money for him to attend camp. "I just don't know anybody."

The mountains slowed down, and the blur of color became clear shades of hunter and forest green. Endless stands of red maple and white pine trees lined the highway like soldiers standing guard in front of the mountains rising behind them.

"We've talked about that, honey," his mother said.

Jake saw the huge camp sign come into view as the van made the right turn into Oak Bay. He wanted to try once again to talk his mother out of sending him here, but instead he just exhaled loudly.

"Your mother's right, son. You'll meet a friend. Maybe even two. . .or five."

An older man stood next to the gatehouse and waved for the Henrys to stop.

Jake's mom rolled her window down.

"Camper?"

"Jake Henry."

The old man looked back at Jake before consulting his megalist of names. "Henry. . .Henry. . .yes, here it is. . . . Jake, you'll be in Cabin 33 over on Karankawa

Hill. Follow this drive all the way to the end. Thirty-three will be on your right. If you go into the lake, you've gone too far."

No one laughed except for the old man. He waved them on, looking at Jake the whole time as the van passed.

Jake's dad parked next to a blue Dumpster that had the camp's oak tree logo painted in white on the side. Jake grabbed his backpack and got out of the car. The sooner he got going, the sooner this whole camp thing could end.

The cabins were painted chocolate brown with white trim around the eaves and doors. Boys and girls of all shapes and sizes were milling around in front of the cabins as well as in the parking lot. There was even a large beach ball getting punched around in the air by random hands.

Jake's dad also got out of the vehicle and caught up to Jake. His mom stayed in the car, checking Facebook on her phone. She'd told Jake she had to make an important call, but he knew better. Last summer when they dropped him off at the airport for his flight to visit Grandma and Grandpa in New York, his mom had cried and his dad told her to dry the tears. Since then, Jake noticed, she had used the distraction of her phone to avoid emotional situations.

Jake found Cabin 33 tucked away behind the other cabins, down a well-worn path that skirted the lake. Boys were running in and out of the screen door. A young guy with an Oak Bay T-shirt and khaki shorts stood on the deck, smiling.

"Hey, guys! Welcome. I'm Sam. I'll be your counselor this week."

Jake noticed that Sam had a cross tattoo on the inside of his right forearm.

"Martin Henry. This is my son, Jake." Jake's dad shook Sam's hand and then said, "His buddy Danny was supposed to be here but got sick at the last minute."

"Sorry about your friend," Sam said. "Trust me, Jake. You're still going to have a blast!"

The happy counselor led Jake and his dad into the cabin. There were bunk beds against three of the four walls. One set of bunks was empty. "Make yourself at home. We're going to meet out front at five. That gives you about an hour to hang out. Meet the guys. After the meeting, we'll all head over to the lodge for dinner."

Jake's dad gave him a quick hug and told him to have a good week. Jake watched his father leave and then thought about his next move. None of the boys who had been in the cabin were left. They all must have slipped out while the counselor was talking.

Jake wanted to just lie on his bunk and wait until dinner to move. But that wouldn't be a smart way to meet anyone.

He walked outside and noticed a bunch of boys had grouped up in front of the cabin. One of them had a football in his hands. Jake walked over to them and saw that the kid with the football was dividing the group into two teams. By the time he was done, all the boys had been sorted except Jake.

That was awkward. None of the boys acknowledged him. They just hustled over to the field and started their game.

Jake walked to where another group of boys were huddled around a camper who was playing a Nintendo Switch game. None of them said anything to Jake, so he said, "Hi." One of the kids said, "Hey," but never made eye contact. This was going to be a long week.

The lake looked like a good option. There were two boys standing by the water's edge skipping stones. Jake headed in that direction. As soon as he got to them, they stopped what they were doing and walked away.

Maybe I smell like a dead skunk.

Jake sat down on a rock and wondered what it would be like to be one of the popular kids. To have the feeling of fitting in and having tons of friends. He watched the sunrays sparkle across the water. Back at school, Danny was his only friend—and even that title was probably a stretch. They didn't hang out after school or on the weekends.

He hadn't even known Danny that long. When Jake's older brother, Ted, moved away to college last August, his parents had decided a change was in order. After the Christmas holidays, they moved with Jake from their country house in Oklahoma to a quaint town house in Charlotte. Right in the middle of the school year.

While Jake and his parents were unpacking, Danny and his mother paid a visit, welcoming them to the neighborhood. Jake had a really hard time connecting with Danny. The boys had nothing in common, but Jake could tell that Danny tried very hard to make him feel welcomed. The camp trip was Jake's mom's idea. She'd told Danny's mother, who in turn said her son would love to go before she even asked him. Danny said he'd go and then managed to get a stomach bug. He was probably faking it just to get out of coming here.

Jake found a small flat stone and sent it skimming

over the lake. He watched it bounce three times before disappearing under the glittering surface. He looked at his watch. He still had thirty minutes before he had to be back at the cabin.

He thought about taking a long walk in the woods, but the warm sun made him sleepy, so he decided to lie down in the grass and rest until it was time to head back.

ooooo

"Open his eyes."

The sound of a man's deep voice came from behind Jake. But when he sat up and turned around to see who was talking, there was no one there.

Just the trees.

And the path that led back to the cabins.

I'm hearing things, that's all.

Then Jake turned back to look at the lake and felt his heart rate explode. It was gone. No water. The only thing he could see was flat land stretching out toward the horizon. Tall grass covered the earth. It swayed back and forth like waves on a wide green sea. The sky was painted with morning tones of dark blue, orange, and red.

The camp had disappeared. The lake, gone. The path, gone. The trees, gone. Oak Bay had simply vanished.

Insane.

CHAPTER 2

1400 B.C.

JERICHO

Vanished. Everything had disappeared, just like that. Gone.

Jake felt a strong breeze at his back, like nature wanted to push him out onto the plain. He turned in circles, feeling small tendrils of fear begin to creep their way across his mind. This wasn't a dream. He hadn't fallen asleep by the lake.

What is this?

Where am I?

The breeze was stronger now. Jake *had* to find the camp. He took off jogging. The wind, growing even more powerful, made it hard to run. At some point, his brain caught up with his body and he realized there was no camp where he knew it should have been.

Jake turned again and looked way off in the distance

where the plain touched the sky. He noticed lines and angles of stone that were dotted with openings, like windows and doors. Tiny shapes moved back and forth like ants across the scene.

He started jogging again, but this time the wind was at his back.

Closer now, the whole arrangement of staggered structures became clearer. The ants were actually people! The entirety of what Jake saw had to be the outline of some massive city that looked like it had been chiseled out of the side of a mountain by a giant sculptor.

Surely someone there would be able to help him get back to the camp.

Coming even closer, he saw a ring of two stone walls running around the base of the city. The first wall rose up from the plain. Behind it there was a grass embankment that looked like the outfield of a baseball diamond. At the crest of that rose the second wall, Jake guessed almost fifty feet above the first one.

In the lower wall were two stone towers on either side of a wide entrance. Each tower had a single wooden door attached to it at the base. A gateway into the city. Jake headed there and thought about the camp guard who had stared at him when they drove onto the camp property. What if there was a guard here? What would Jake say? *Can you help me get back to Oak Bay?*

To Jake's relief, there was no guard. Just past the entrance, the ground angled up a steep incline covered in grass. At the top of the hill, he saw a boy who looked to be about his age standing behind a group of kids. Jake couldn't tell what the kids were doing, but it seemed clear they weren't involving the boy in the back.

The kid turned around and saw Jake; then he took off running.

"Hey, wait!" Jake took off after the kid.

He followed the boy along the grass until he came to an opening in the second, inner wall. The grass turned into a stone path that led through the outskirts of the walled city. Jake ran past houses that were carved into the outer wall. As he ran, he noticed that off to his left the inner wall rose much higher than the outer wall. Even way up there, more houses had been created.

The boy stopped and cut through an opening in between two houses, and Jake followed.

The alley ended in a doorway. The boy ran in the door. Jake followed. There was hardly any light inside, only patches of sunlight that poured down from somewhere way up above.

But the lack of light didn't keep the boy from running. He navigated the twists and turns of darkened stone like a nimble and swift cat. Jake had a hard time keeping up. It felt like he was running through houses and hallways, but the sporadic shards of light every once in a while made it hard to know for certain. Jake kept running into walls and stumbling over rocks. He would have lost the kid completely if it hadn't been for an old man who suddenly appeared in his path.

"Dair! Stop!"

The boy stopped. Jake ran up and stopped behind the boy.

The boy turned on Jake. "Are you with Ka'nah?"

"Who?"

The boy stared at Jake, disbelief in his eyes. "Why are you chasing me?"

The old man put a hand on the boy's shoulder. "Dair, let him speak. He's not from around here. And he's obviously not an enemy spy, because I've never seen anything like what he's wearing. Let's listen to what he has to say."

"Yes, Levi."

Jake took his cue and explained how he'd found himself in this place. "I just need help getting back. I'm supposed to be back at my cabin. I don't want to miss dinner."

The boy's face changed from the hard lines of fear into a soft smile of greeting. "My name's Dair."

"Can you tell me about Ka'nah?"

Dair continued. "He is a wicked man. The meanest man in Jericho."

"Jericho? Like the Bible Jericho?"

"The *what*?"

Jake shook his head. "Never mind." There was no way on earth he could actually be back in the real Jericho of the Bible.

"Let's go," Levi said. The old man walked away, and Dair followed him. Jake did the same. After a few more minutes of navigating dim stone alleyways, Jake felt the ground angle up. They climbed a huge flight of stone steps that took them to the second, upper level of Jericho. Levi led the boys out across a ledge that skirted the houses built around the edge of the upper wall. The old man stopped at a small wooden door. Dair inched past Levi and opened it, letting in a flood of daylight.

Jake squinted and then followed Levi and Dair through the opening and out onto an expansive stone walkway. They were somewhere way high up on the top of the city. So high, in fact, that Jake freaked out. He hated heights, and this was crazy high. Higher than the

Mind Bender at Six Flags. That ridiculous roller coaster, the one his dad forced him to go on, was the memory his brain was choosing to bring back now.

They had gone on vacation, and his dad said he was going to make Jake ride the coaster to force him to face his fear. The whole debacle of plunging down an insane three-story drop and then around two inverted loops in a tiny car only served to solidify Jake's terror of being anywhere off the ground. Jake tried facing his fear that day but lost the fight.

A loud sound like thunder boomed up over the stone walls. Jake jumped in response. "What in the world was that?"

Dair stared at Jake. "What are you called?"

"My name is Jake. Jake Henry."

"Well, Jakehenry. That noise is the sound of the city gates closing. There is a threat to our safety out on the plains. Come here." Dair stepped to the edge of the walkway. "Look."

Jake forced himself to stand next to Dair. His legs felt weak with the fear of being up so high. He looked down and saw a sea of people flooding the plain. Thousands and thousands marching toward the city. He thought about the Bible story. The Israelites marched against Jericho. Yes, they marched around the city once a day for six days, and on the seventh day. . .

This whole city is going to be destroyed!

"Have they marched around your city at all?" Jake had to know where he was on the timeline of events.

"They have not," Levi answered. "Until now, they've just stayed out there on the plain."

Jake was trapped.

The gates were shut.

And there was no way out.

CHAPTER 3

There were thousands of men holding weapons. Even though he was so high up, Jake could see that the men in front of the procession were dressed in robes and carrying horns. Behind them, there was something that looked like a big golden box. It was so shiny that it appeared to be glowing. Jake thought about the story and remembered that that was the ark of the covenant! The presence of God.

"Listen, Dair. I need to tell you something."

"What?"

"We need to get out of here."

"Why? This is Jericho. Nothing's going to happen to this city."

Jake considered his options, but there weren't any others. All he could do was warn Dair. "That army down there..."

"What about it?"

"They're going to march around your city for six days and then—"

Dair looked at Jake with wide eyes. "Then what?"

"Then on the seventh day, the whole city is going to be destroyed."

Dair laughed.

"I'm serious. On the seventh day, all the walls are going to collapse and that army is going to take over the city. Everyone is going to be wiped out."

"Do you know how crazy that sounds?"

"I know, but you have to believe me. I don't understand what I'm doing here, but you—and everyone in this city—are in big trouble."

Dair placed a hand on Jake's shoulder. "I don't know what you're doing here either, but I have to go now."

Jake still had questions. "Can you at least help me get out of here?"

"Even if I did get you out, there's no way you'd survive out there in the wilderness."

"Maybe if I get back to the same spot I was out on the plain, I can get back to my time."

Dair smiled. "Come on."

He took off toward the opening they had just come

out of, and Jake followed.

But before they got to the door, a giant man stepped from the shadows of the doorway, blocking their path.

Dair tried to change directions, but the man was too fast. His hand shot out and grabbed Dair's shirt. "I am very sad that you wanted to leave our family."

Jake couldn't believe how tall the man was.

"Who's your new friend? Is he the reason you ran away?" The man dragged Dair across the top of the stone wall until they were both inches away from Jake.

Jake looked for a way out. He started to run down the wall, away from the giant man, but a second man wielding a sword stepped onto the wall, blocking his escape. Jake was in a pickle.

The man kept his hand on Dair. "Who are you?"

Jake noticed the man's eyes. The irises seemed to spark, like green circles of electricity. "I'm Jake."

"Hello, Jake. I'm really glad you're here." The words weren't all the way out of his mouth when Jake felt a powerful hand grab him. "You will make a perfect addition to the family."

Jake tried to resist, but the man was too powerful.

The man dragged both boys off the wall, through the same opening they came through earlier, and down the long flight of stone stairs. When they reached the bottom of the stairs, Dair told his captor to let Jake go. "He doesn't belong here."

The sinister man grinned. "All the more reason for Ka'nah to meet him. Let's go."

He pulled the boys out of the dark passage into the light. Jake looked around and saw groups of people gathered and talking to one another. Behind the people were stands, displaying all kinds of foods that Jake guessed were fruit.

How come no one is trying to stop this guy? Can't they see we don't want to go with him?

Jake tried to think of a way to escape the man's clutches. Why wasn't Dair yelling for help? Well, he could!

"Help!"

But instead of answering Jake's plea, the people just stared at him and then turned back to their discussions.

"Young man, please don't waste your breath or time. Everyone in this city is on my side because I serve Ka'nah. Even the king does my—"

Before the evil one could finish his thought, a wooden cane flew in and struck the man's arm that was holding Jake.

"RUN!"

ooooo

Jake looked down and saw that the man had let go of him, but not Dair. He didn't have time to stand around. "Dair, I'll come back and get you. Hang in there!"

Before the evil one could stop him, Jake took off running.

ooooo

Jake saw that the sun was a lot lower in the sky now. He had to have been running for more than an hour. He didn't think Jericho was that big, but it must have been, because he was still inside the walls.

He blinked, half hoping that the lake and campground would now be in front of him. The other half of his hope knew better and wasn't surprised when his eyes opened to the massive walls of Jericho, still rising all around him. Strangely, Jake didn't feel fear—that unworthy sensation borne from a lack of confidence—at the idea of having to rescue Dair. Rather, the opposite was true. Jake felt strength flow through his veins as he thought about his purpose here. He had to get his new friend out from the evil clutches of the leader named Ka'nah.

The question was, how could one young boy outwit a grown man whose talent was reaping evil? From where

Jake sat on top of the jagged roofline, he had a random thought from his fifth-grade science teacher, Mrs. Myers. She was big on slowing down and making observations. Jake remembered a day last fall. Mrs. Myers came into class wearing a firefighter outfit. When the kids asked her why she was dressed that way, she said she wanted to talk about making observations.

She said it was very easy to take things around us for granted, even crazy things such as fire hydrants. She asked the class to write down how many fire hydrants they thought there were between their homes and the school. They all wrote down their guesses. Jake couldn't remember seeing any but guessed two. He remembered Mrs. Myers giving the class a brief lecture on how fires were fought in the early days. There were bucket brigades that would move water from cisterns to the site of the fire, one bucket at a time. It was, according to Mrs. Myers, very tedious. She said that sometime around 1801, the fire hydrant was invented.

The next day, the class reported back their findings. All the kids were blown away by just how many fire hydrants they saw once they actually paid attention and were looking for them.

Because of Mrs. Myers, Jake forced himself to look

past the obvious and make deep observations of the city he had been trapped in. Jericho.

How was he supposed to figure out where Dair was? After a good long while of taking mental notes of the paths he'd taken and the different types of structures he'd seen, Jake was more frustrated now than he was earlier when his new friend had been captured. There simply wasn't a way for Jake to know where Dair had been taken.

Unless. . .

He had to talk to Levi. The old man would know whether his idea would work. After all, he had saved Jake with one stroke of a cane.

Jake ran back through the twists and turns of the city, headed to Levi's. He wished he knew what Ka'nah looked like so he could keep his eye out for him, but Jake had to have faith that he was here for a reason. *God, please help me get to Levi's house without getting caught.*

Jake navigated the stone streets and narrow passages between buildings that loomed over him like a slumbering dragon. Careful not to stir the beast, Jake hurried through Jericho always looking over his shoulder for fear of getting caught. Eventually he made his way to the old man's house, sat down on the stoop, and waited.

Time passed, along with many people.

At sunset, Levi returned. He noticed Jake sitting on the stone porch and waved.

Jake stood to greet him. "Will you help me?"

"Of course, child. Haven't I already helped?" Levi shuffled past Jake and led him into a very primitive home. "I will tell you right now, you will not be able to beat Ka'nah. Many before you have tried, but none were successful."

"I have to try."

Levi nodded in approval. "Yes, young Jake Henry. That's all any of us can do."

Jake shared his idea with the old man. "I can wear a cloak like the people who bring in the daily fruit supply. I'll hide a second cloak at the bottom of my fruit basket. Once I'm in, I'll find Dair and give him the extra cloak."

Levi looked at Jake.

"We'll walk right out the front gate."

Levi walked away and came back a few minutes later with a handful of small brown fruit. "We must do it quickly. I was followed. It won't be long before Ka'nah's men come looking for us."

"What about my idea? Do you think it will work?"

"It might, but you'll need a miracle to help you."

CHAPTER 4

The old man shuffled across the dirt floor of his modest stone dwelling. He took a date from the handful he had been carrying and offered it to Jake.

Jake took the fruit and was surprised at how sweet it tasted.

Levi ate a date himself and then stood at his entryway. He looked out at the city as he spoke.

"Ka'nah was known as a *gibbor*, one of great might. Like the great fortress walls you see outside that make up our city, young Ka'nah spoke powerful words to the people and made them believe he was some sort of messiah."

Jake couldn't believe what was happening to him. He wondered what was happening back at camp. He was a little freaked out that he was somehow experiencing this old Bible story, but he felt comfortable here in Jericho nonetheless.

"Would you like another date?" Levi was still facing out toward the city.

Jake didn't want to be rude, but he really would be okay if he never ate another. "No, thank you."

Now Levi turned around to face his guest. "Ka'nah's parents were poor. They always had to work hard to afford even the smallest meal, and then they became very sick and passed away. This forced Ka'nah to live on the streets. He somehow found enough food to survive."

Jake stood and met Levi in the doorway. "I don't mean to be rude, but your entire city is going to be destroyed. I don't think we should stay here. We need to find a way to get Dair, and then we need to leave."

Levi laughed. "Son, nothing's going to happen to Jericho." He shuffled out into the sunlight. Jake followed reluctantly. He wondered if it was a bad move coming here to get the man's help.

"Sir, it's true. Did you see those people marching around the city earlier today? They're going to march around it for the next six days. On the seventh day, they'll march around it seven times and then the people will shout and all these walls are going to fall."

"You know how ridiculous that sounds, right?"

Jake thought about it from Levi's perspective. It did sound ridiculous.

"Young man, I saw the people marching, but I also see you. So, what is clear to me is that you've been sent to save us from them."

Jake had to try to convince the guy he was wrong. "Sir—"

"Just Levi."

"Okay. Levi."

"Go on." The old man moved his weathered right hand in a circular motion like Jake had done in science class. Mrs. Myers called it *wafting*.

"I'm not here to protect you from the people walking around your city. In fact, I have no idea how I got here or why I'm here. The only thing I do know is that those folks are going to march around the walls seven times in a few days. . . ."

Levi lifted both hands.

Jake stopped talking. He used the pause to recall more details from the Jericho story.

"Boy, where are you coming up with these bizarre ideas?"

"The Bible."

"The *what*?"

31

Jake gave a brief description of the Bible and waited for the information to sink in.

"Even though I have never heard of a Bible, it's disturbing how you claim to know future events." Levi looked shocked. "Young man, if you're not here to stop the crowd marching, then maybe you've been sent to put an end to Ka'nah."

Jake closed his eyes for a second. When he opened them, Levi had turned to face him. "Sir, uh, I mean, Levi. I really have no idea what I'm doing here. I did feel a connection to Dair. Dair got captured by Ka'nah, and I want to help get him out."

"Okay," Levi said. "Let me finish telling you about my old friend and maybe we can come up with a plan to get Dair back."

Jake listened as his new mentor talked about how Ka'nah went from stealing food to survive to stealing food to thrive. He listened as Levi explained how Ka'nah gathered other street kids to steal for him, eventually giving them part of his growing cache.

"He came to me one night right here and took me to the edge of the city wall. He knew I was poor, and he wanted to help me. I let him for a while, but then I saw how the wealth was changing him. Ka'nah quickly became selfish and arrogant. Soon the joke was, even though our city had an appointed king, everyone knew who the real king was."

Jake didn't know how all this was going to help get Dair rescued. He waited patiently as Levi recounted more facts about Ka'nah's descent into a life of darkness. Then, when Jake was sure the old man would keep talking forever, he stopped and asked a question.

"Young Jake, do you think you have a purpose in life?"

"Uh, I guess."

"Do you believe you were created for a reason?"

"I don't know. Back home, I'm nobody. People ignore me. I'm not looking for a pity party, it just doesn't feel too good."

"That's a lot coming from someone as young as yourself. No one is a mistake. Do you understand me?"

Jake raised his eyes, shocked at how animated Levi had become. "Yes, sir. But, like I said, I came to you for help rescuing Dair. After that, I need your help getting out of this city, because in a few days this whole place is going to be destroyed, and I'd rather be far away from here when that happens."

Levi lifted his hands and put them on either side of Jake's face. "If this place is going to be destroyed, why bother trying to save Dair?"

"Well, after I save him, I was hoping you could get all three of us out of here before it all falls apart."

"I've got an even better idea. Why don't we help all the kids escape?"

Jake loved the idea. "Like Harriet Tubman and the Underground Railroad."

"What?"

"Never mind."

"Okay, it's late, and you need to sleep. I will stay up and perfect your plan to get you into Ka'nah's compound. I'll also think about how we can get all the kids out, and then I'll show you how to get out of the city."

"Thank you!"

Jake felt like a new person here in Jericho. Here he had a friend, and here he had a purpose. He held an ounce of worry about not being able to get back to camp, but it wasn't overwhelming. Here in Jericho, Jake felt like he mattered.

Levi led him to a spot where Jake got down on the floor and put his head on a folded quilt. *God, thank You for being with me and giving me a friend. Thank You for Levi. Please help me get Dair. In Jesus' name.*

Trying to go to sleep was hard. Jake was excited

that, even though it took coming to this faraway place, he finally felt like he had a purpose. He loved feeling connected to Levi and Dair. He embraced the feeling of not being alone anymore!

He could stay in Jericho forever but knew this place wouldn't be around too much longer. He hoped for some much-needed sleep and courage to rescue Dair and the others.

He wondered what was going on back at camp. Were the counselors looking for him? Did anyone care? How long had he been gone? Would they have called his parents by now? Was time the same here in Jericho as it was back home? The endless flood of questions filled Jake's mind, and at last it made him sleepy. At some point, he gave up questioning things and gave in to the weariness that had overtaken his body.

Lord, please watch over me.

Help me get home.

Amen.

CHAPTER 5

Jake opened his eyes. Dream fragments danced in his head. They were like scrambled puzzle pieces just dumped out of the box, begging to be sorted and put together to display the picture they were meant to show.

He started sorting. . . .

Some of the dream pieces made Jake remember being lifted off the ground and carried somewhere. Other dream pieces came together and reminded him of being placed in a dark place where light couldn't enter. The last bits came back to him in the form of sound. Muffled voices and objects shattering.

But even with his eyes open, the world was still black. He felt the hard ground beneath him and tried to think about where he was. He felt rested but couldn't see anything. Maybe he was still dreaming.

He pushed himself up to a sitting position. From this

new angle he could see a thin sliver of light cutting its way into the shadows and landing on a rock opposite it. He put a hand on the light and felt the stone it was pointing to. He found that the rock moved. Using both hands, he slid the stone back and squinted at the light shining behind it.

When he got his bearings, Jake saw that he had been sleeping in a hidden alcove. Levi must have shut the door after Jake fell asleep. So the dream had become reality. . . .

"Levi?"

The first thing Jake noticed was that the ceramic bowl Levi had pulled the dates from was smashed to pieces all over the floor.

"Levi?"

Still no answer.

Jake got up and walked around the tiny house and found no sign of the old man. In the middle of the broken pieces of the clay bowl, he saw something shiny. He bent down and saw that it was small, round, and golden, like a coin. He picked it up and turned it over in his hand. On one side it had a big tree with fruit like apples all over it, and on the other side was the letter *K*. Jake noticed that the *K* had a snake coiled around it.

Ka'nah?

Jake put the coin in his pocket and cautiously stepped outside. The faint light told him it was still very early morning. He looked around to see if anyone was watching. When he felt confident that no one was around, he headed off in the direction of the rooftop where he'd last seen Dair.

ooooo

Jake made his way to the section of the city where the wall houses rose the highest. After a few flights of stone stairways, he made it to the roof. He crept to the edge and marveled at the awesome view of the wide-open plain below. From the position of the sun, he made a mental note that he was facing east. He looked down and saw the main city gate he had entered yesterday.

The plain was empty, with no sign of the marching Israelites. It was probably too early for them to be marching.

Jake picked up a small pebble from the ground. He decided this would be how he would keep up with the number of days the Israelites marched around the city. Because on the seventh day. . .

Someone was walking up beside him. Jake turned and saw a young girl, no older than eight or nine, standing there. The poor kid looked like she hadn't bathed or changed clothes in forever. Her black hair was a tangled mess, and her light brown skin looked like it had been gift wrapped in dirt. She wore a baggy shirt and loose-fitting pants that were held up by a rope tied around her skinny waist.

Looking closer, Jake noticed the girl had the same *K* marking on her pants that Jake had seen on the coin. He guessed the girl belonged to Ka'nah. This wasn't right. The man didn't have the right to make children do his evil work. He had to get Dair out.

"I'm Jake. Who are you?"

The girl just stared.

The sound of a faraway train came on the wind, making Jake forget about the girl and wonder what could make the noise since trains didn't exist yet. The rumbling grew louder. Jake looked back down to the plain and saw the wave of people coming around the southeast corner walls. The Israelites were marching again. Jake picked up a second pebble from the roof and dropped it in his pocket with the other one.

Two down, five to go.

"Ka'nah?" Jake pointed to the *K* on the kid's pants.

The girl considered Jake's question. She nodded.

"What's your name?"

"Ruth," the girl said.

"Hi, Ruth." Jake thought for a second. "Do you know Levi?"

Another nod.

"Levi sent you to meet me?"

A smile.

"Okay, Levi sent you. Now what?"

With that, the girl turned and took off. Jake followed.

They crossed the uneven rooftops of Jericho in a counterclockwise direction. The girl was agile. Jake thought the kid was half gazelle, the way she jumped and climbed as they went. Although he was tired, Jake kept up. When they came to a roof that he guessed was in the northwest corner of the city, they stopped.

"This is Ka'nah's base."

Jake made a fist and yanked it back. *Score!*

"Levi said you might need help."

Jake shrugged his shoulders. "I don't know what's going on." He gave Ruth a short summary of how one minute he had been sitting by the lake in North Carolina and the next he was walking into the great walled city of Jericho.

"Let me tell you something. I believe everything

happens for a reason. Levi told me you have a connection with my friend Dair."

"Yes! When I got here, I saw him being ignored by a large group of kids. It was the same thing that was happening to me back at the camp I told you about."

Jake could tell Ruth considered his words. She pointed down to the section of the city she called the base. "Down there are more kids who feel like you do. Ignored and pretty much forgotten. Ka'nah helps us feel wanted."

Jake looked down at the area Ruth indicated. More stone houses rising from the dusty ground with a large rectangular plot of land that was empty. It made Jake think of a soccer field. Boys and girls were walking back and forth across it, carrying bags. When they got to the end of the field that was farthest away from where Jake and Ruth stood, they dumped out the contents of the sacks. It looked like all sorts of items appeared: fruit, pottery, fabric, and other things that Jake couldn't make out. "Ruth, what are they doing?"

"Unloading. That stuff down there is all stolen. First, it all gets sorted. Then a team hauls it into a bunch of storehouses. Then different shops around the city will put in orders. Runners will take the supplies to those shops."

Jake interrupted. "Like FedEx?"

"Fed *what*?"

"Sorry, wrong century. Keep going."

"That's how Ka'nah makes most of his money."

Jake watched as more kids entered the courtyard, each with a heavy burden of stolen goods. "And what is your job?"

Ruth considered her answer for a second before she spoke. "I'm a collector."

Jake could only imagine what that meant. "A collector of what?"

"People."

Jake's silence was enough to keep Ruth talking.

"Like you, Jake. I'm here to take you back home."

"North Carolina?"

"What?"

"North Carolina. It's home for me, and you said you would take me there."

Ruth looked at Jake. "Not sure what North Carolina is, but I mean *home* as in down there in Ka'nah's base."

"Do you know where Dair is?"

"Yes, and the only way you will be able to see him is if you join the others and gather. Ka'nah has watchers all around the city, looking for new family members. Don't turn around, but there's a man behind us holding a stick. He's a watcher. If you are seen gathering, and if you're good at it, he will invite you back to the base. That's when you will have the chance to meet Ka'nah and be given a place to stay."

"Gathering? You mean *stealing*, right?"

"Jake, I don't know how things work in your world, but here in Jericho we are trying to keep everything equal."

"In my world, stealing is illegal."

Ruth walked away, inviting Jake to follow, and headed toward a section of the roof that gave them a broader view of the action down in the base. "That's where your friend is."

Jake squinted and could barely make out the figures of children digging through one of the unloaded piles.

Jake was confused. "I don't get it. How can this crazy place be better than your own homes?"

"Jake," Ruth said, "all of us working for Ka'nah share a story. All of us were unwanted."

"What do you mean?"

"I think you know what I mean. *Ignored. Pushed to the side.*"

Jake watched one of the kids grab something covered

in gold and lift it high above his head. A handful of other boys and girls who had been rummaging through the other piles stopped what they were doing and made their way over to see what their friend had found.

"Come on, Jake. We can't stay here. Would you like to join our family and find your friend?"

"Ruth, I'm starting to freak out a little bit. I don't know why I'm here, and I'm glad you're talking to me, but I'm not joining a group who steals."

Ruth started slowly walking away from Jake. "I understand. Good luck." And as the last word was spoken, the girl took off in a sprint toward the base.

Jake looked back to the base and saw the kids were now in a circle around the boy, arms outstretched, trying to grab the golden object that was still in his hands. Jake did want to be down there, a part of the action. He did want to help Dair escape. He took the two pebbles out of his pocket and held one in each hand. He thought about how this whole city would be a massive pile of rubble soon. He had to get Dair out.

Jake clutched the pebbles and started making his way down the twisting paths in the direction of the base. When he had gone a good distance from where he started, he turned to see if there was a man following him.

Just as Ruth had said, Jake saw a man holding a big stick behind him. The man had muscles big enough to make John Cena proud. This was the miracle that Levi said Jake would need to get into the compound. He wouldn't need a cloak and a fruit basket. Jake just needed to make a decision.

Jake put his pebbles back in his pocket and continued making his way down rock corridors and alleyways. When he reached the ground level, he saw the wall that hid Ka'nah's base.

"Help."

A weak voice came to Jake. He looked down and saw a bald-headed old man holding a large bowl filled with what looked like the dates that Levi had last night. Next to the old man was an open cloth sack that was filled with coins. Jake looked at the man's face and noticed a big scar that cut across his right cheek.

I have to rescue Dair.

"Can you please help? My wife is very sick." The old man held up the plate of fruit. "Please."

Jake studied the man's face, committing the scar and bald head to memory. "Forgive me. I promise I'll bring it back." Before the old man could ask what he meant, Jake swiped the money bag and took off running. He found an alcove to duck into and catch his breath. Bent over, Jake felt someone standing over him.

"Welcome to the family."

It was John Cena.

CHAPTER 6

The man's grip was like a pit bull latched onto Jake's arm. He pulled Jake through a small entryway in the main wall and finally let go.

"Follow me."

Jake still clutched the money bag and had no problem obeying. He followed the strong man across the dirt courtyard and into a large stone structure that reminded him of one of those old church buildings from puzzles and country towns. The only difference was that the building didn't have a steeple.

Inside, there was a buzz of activity. Boys and girls holding big bags scurried back and forth while grown men and women sat on long benches that ran all along the perimeter of the building. The strong man guided Jake through the crowd to a small opening in the far corner.

Now Jake found himself in a chamber that had a window cut out in the side wall that let enough light in to see. Unlike the other room, this one had only one person, a man with long black hair that came to his back, sitting on a bench. He was wrapped in a heavy cloak that matched the color of his hair. He had a very thick beard that reached all the way to his chest. Jake knew who he was without being told.

"Hello, Jake. Levi told me all about you. So glad you could join us."

The John Cena dude stood off to Jake's left.

"Here's my first bag of money." Jake held the money bag up in front of him so Ka'nah could get a good look at it.

The leader stood. "I don't need your money. In fact, I would like to give you a gift for being brave enough to join us." Ka'nah walked over to a table that was covered in bags. He picked one up and handed it to Jake. "Add this to the one you came in with as a little something to begin your savings. Nathal here will show you where to store it in the vault. I look forward to hearing about your progress."

He started to leave through the door Jake had entered.

"Wait!" The command escaped Jake's mouth before he could think about whether it was smart to say.

"Excuse me?" The robed leader stopped and trained his dark eyes on Jake. "I'm the one who gives the orders here. I'll let this go, considering that you are brand new and do not understand the rules."

Jake thought about Dair and Levi. He thought about the lake back at camp and how he should be there loading up a plate with french fries and an extra-large glob of ketchup. If this was just a bad dream, then Jake was not about to start worrying about *rules*. "Where's Dair?"

Ka'nah looked at Nathal. "He actually stole the money bag?"

The bodyguard nodded.

Ka'nah shook his head. "Young Jake, I like you. You're not afraid to challenge the boundaries set before you. Your friend is in the sleeping hall. Go there yourself, and get some rest. Tomorrow will be a very busy day."

The man didn't wait for a reply. He strolled out the same way Jake had entered the chamber. Nathal led Jake and his two money bags out a new doorway and down a long flight of stone stairs. When the stairs ended, Jake followed the bodyguard down a long, dim hallway illuminated by only a single candle that rested on a small wooden table. Nathal grabbed the candle and continued on through the stone corridor.

"What is going to happen tomorrow?" Jake wondered where on earth he was being taken and figured getting the man to talk might bring some answers.

"Master is leading the biggest gathering ever. The whole city will feel our presence."

They walked through another small doorway and stood in a room that had tables set up in rows. Jake guessed this was their dining hall. He didn't feel like asking the guard any more questions.

After navigating a second hallway, one much shorter than the first, Jake followed Nathal into another room, this one square in design. In the middle of the chamber stood a man at least three times the size of Jake's current keeper. The guy reminded him of Drax the Destroyer from *Guardians of the Galaxy*. The walls were lined with shelves, and the shelves were lined with money bags.

Drax looked at Jake and raised a hand, palm open. "Welcome. This is the vault. Your money is safe with me."

Jake handed his bags over and watched the behemoth place them on the end of a shelf close to the entry at the far end of the chamber. "Thanks."

Jake wondered who all the other bags belonged to,

and how did Drax keep it all straight?

"Come," Nathal said. "I will take you to your room."

On the way out of the vault, Jake made a mental note where his money bags were located. Leaving the chamber through a different door, he followed Nathal out into another narrow passageway. They weren't in this one very long before entering a new door.

"This is where everyone rests. Your room is on the upper level."

The guide took Jake up a long flight of steps that curved around in a circle. It was very cramped. Jake was grateful they weren't on the stairs for long.

Nathal waited on the landing for Jake to catch up. When Jake made it to the upper floor, his guide led him down a hallway that was crowded with groups of boys and men. Some were standing, while others sat. They stared at Jake like he was some alien armed with a weapon that would annihilate them all. Jake scanned their faces, trying to find Dair.

"Your room is down here." Nathal stopped when he made it to the end of the hallway. He pointed to the last room on the left. Jake noticed that none of the rooms had doors. He went into his room and cringed. There was one window, which was like the other one back where he had first met Ka'nah—nothing more than a square hole in the wall. No glass covered the windows here. There was nothing else in the room. The stone floor would serve as Jake's bed.

Jake went to the window and could see the dirt yard on the far side of the compound. Closer, just below his window, was another courtyard. This one looked more like a garden of two dead trees and a wild array of bushes that were silently screaming for a drink.

"We have a meeting in the main yard at dusk. I will come back and get you." Nathal nodded and left.

Jake stared at the two trees and wondered about camp again. How would he get back there? Would he go to bed on the hard floor, close his eyes, and somehow get back to North Carolina? Even though a part of him was afraid and confused, Jake actually felt like he had a purpose here in Jericho. There were things going on here that needed his help fixing. He felt a strange connection to Dair and a clear desire to help get him out of this bizarre compound.

Boys of all ages shuffled past Jake's open door. There were conversations that Jake didn't understand and others that he caught bits and pieces of that were mostly about who had captured the most treasure. Somewhere in the middle of what he could understand and what he could not, Jake clearly heard the name *Levi*. Jake jumped to the doorway.

"Levi?" As Jake said the old man's name, he scanned the faces closest to him to see if any of the boys would show a reaction. The conversations stopped, and the hall fell to silence. The boys looked at Jake as if they were trying to figure out how he knew Levi.

"I met him yesterday," Jake said to the staring faces. "We are friends." That part was a stretch, but Jake didn't know what else to say.

A young boy stepped from the group.

"He's in the bad place."

CHAPTER 7

Jake had to squat to be eye level with the boy. "What's the bad place?"

"We call it the Blood Mountain. It's on the far side of our city. There's a small opening that leads to a tiny ledge. The ledge looks down over the plain, but there's no path. Just jagged rocks that rise up like blades of the fiercest warriors. When a person is exiled, they are sent to the ledge and not let back in. The strong ones think they can make it down the treacherous cliff, but soon find out they are not just fighting the rocks. Birds of prey quickly find them too weak to defend themselves. The winged ones have figured out that a few quick strikes will eventually make the people fall. The birds are patient and continue the strikes. After that, when they know there will be no more fight, the birds feast and spill the blood of the man over the hillside."

Jake tried to process what the boy was saying. "How do I get to the ledge?"

"It's no use. Even if you got there, Ka'nah has it guarded from the inside. That big man you saw in the vault has a twin brother who guards the door that leads to the ledge."

Jake had no way of winning that fight. He put Levi on hold for a minute. "How about Dair? Does anyone know him?"

The boy who had been talking to Jake looked back at the group of boys. He pointed to a tall boy standing near the back of the huddle. "He's Dair's brother!"

Jake smiled and introduced himself. "Hey. I met your brother yesterday. He was showing me around when Ka'nah's men showed up and took him away."

"Yes, Dair was trying to get back home to check on our sister. She was being bothered by some people in the city. He didn't return when he said he would, so he was tracked down and brought back here."

"Where is he now?" Jake hoped the kid wasn't going to say Blood Mountain.

"Under the vault."

"Under the vault?"

The tall boy stepped forward, pushing the smaller

boy aside. "Here, let me show you." He went into Jake's room and stepped up to the window. Jake followed. The boy pointed down toward the dying garden.

Jake looked but wasn't sure what the kid was pointing to.

"The two trees. Look to the right of them, on the ground. Do you see it?"

Jake looked in the spot he thought the kid was talking about but didn't see anything out of the ordinary. "No. What am I looking for?"

"That line of green. See it?"

Jake adjusted his line of sight. "Yes."

"It's the only part they keep watered. It marks a hidden entrance to the vault."

"Dair is under there?" Jake asked.

"No. He's under the vault. The vault serves two purposes. The one that you probably saw on the way in here is the part where treasure is stored. The other vault, below that one, is where people are kept for punishment. But, if you want to get him out, your only shot is going down that way."

Jake had no idea what was going on. Things here in this otherworld kept getting crazier and crazier.

"And, if you want to try to get him out, I'd go during

the meeting. It's going to start soon. When you see the main courtyard fill with people, that's when you should go."

"Have you tried to get your brother out?"

"No, because if I get caught, Ka'nah will take our whole family and throw us out on the ledge."

Jake had one last question. "What makes you think I can get him out?"

"I don't think you can get him out. But I'd rather you try and fail than not try at all." The boy walked away from the window and left Jake's room.

Jake looked back out the window. He stared at the swath of green that marked the secret entrance to the vault where Dair was being held. There wasn't a choice. He knew he had some connection to Dair and had to do whatever it took to rescue him. *Lord, I don't know what's going on, but You do. I don't understand why I'm experiencing this place. Please help me!*

A horn sounded, deep and rumbling across the compound. It made Jake think of the time he was in Texas visiting his grandparents in Fort Worth. They took him to the zoo, and when they were just inside the main entrance Jake heard the same kind of deep rumbling. His grandfather said it was the male lion roaring. It was a sound that could be heard for miles.

The horn blasted again, and the boys who had been crowded around started leaving. Glancing out the window, Jake saw groups of boys walking out of the dorm and heading across the garden. Farther away, the main courtyard began filling up with kids.

Now was his time to move.

He joined the throng and went down the stairs to the ground floor. But instead of following them toward the front of the compound, Jake split off and headed to the garden where the two trees stood.

"Hey!"

Jake reached the trees and ignored the voice. He saw the green mark.

"Hey! Where are you going?"

Jake decided a show of confidence was in order. "I'm trying to help a friend." He didn't look back.

"Who are you?"

"My name's Jake. Come here and help me get this cover off."

The one asking all the questions gave Jake a once-over and must have decided he was legit. The guy left Jake alone and kept walking.

Jake ran his hand along the green grass beneath the two trees. He found a metal handle attached to a wooden lid. He lifted it up and felt a wave of stale air rush up against his face. It smelled like garbage that had sat in his garage way past the pickup date. Although it was dark, Jake could make out a set of rungs that had been fastened to the wall and led to a black nowhere.

Jake lowered himself into the hole and started down the makeshift ladder.

More darkness waited. It called to him like a lighthouse guiding the sailor home.

As Jake went down, cold air swirled around his body. After about fifty rungs, his feet touched down on solid ground. He couldn't see much except for a small ring around him from the light above that made it this far down the shaft.

In the distance, a small sliver of light cut a white line across the subterranean passage in the black that surrounded him. Still, no one had followed him. Jake stretched out his arms and began shuffling forward toward the light.

Twenty steps didn't bring the slash of light any closer. Jake was confused. Maybe being down in the earth made his mind play tricks on him.

Ten more steps forward.

Ten more.

Light exploded all around, forcing Jake to shut his eyes. He tried opening them again, but all he could see were odd shapes moving around in circles. He shut his eyes a second time. He couldn't see, but he heard something in front of him.

When Jake opened his eyes, a form appeared. The form turned into the outline of a person, who smashed into Jake, knocking him down.

"Jake?"

The voice came in familiar tones. Jake tried shaking the dizzy feeling that came from being plowed into.

"Jake. It's me. Dair!"

Dair?

"Can you hear me?"

Yes. I can hear you.

"Sorry. I wasn't watching where I was going."

Jake realized he hadn't said anything out loud. "Dair."

"Yes, Jake. It's me, Dair."

"Thank goodness. What now?"

"There's something going on at the ledge. Somebody tried to help Levi. The guard from the vault left to help the guard at the ledge. I used his absence to take off, and here I am."

Jake thought about the man out on the streets with

the scar across his face. The one he'd taken the money from. "I need your help. I need to go up into the vault."

"No. We have to hurry and go that way." Dair pointed to the ladder.

Jake quickly explained his plan to Dair.

"Okay, but we must hurry. Come on!"

Jake followed Dair through the underground tunnel until they reached another ladder. Dair went up through the opening in the floor and waved Jake after him. The money storage room was void of the monster guard. Jake scanned the shelves and saw his two bags. He grabbed them and hurried after Dair, who was standing in a different doorway than Jake had come in earlier.

"Come on. This leads to the roof."

Jake continued after Dair, following him up a narrow flight of stairs that opened up on a landing looking down on the main courtyard. He could see the giant guard lumbering back to the vault.

"Let's go!" Dair's voice was filled with hope. He jumped from the landing to an adjacent rooftop, one that was closer to the compound's main entrance. Jake did the same and was grateful he didn't break his legs in the process.

"You okay?"

"Yes, Dair. Where are we going?" Jake hoped that it would be somewhere away from this crazy place.

"There's another set of stairs that leads out to the front entrance."

Jake held tight to the money bags as he ran and jumped across the roofs of Jericho behind Dair. As he ran, he glanced down at the plain far below. He thought about the fact that this whole massive fortress of a city was going to be a pile of rubble in a few days.

"Jake!" Dair yelled. "Look out!"

Jake looked around but didn't know what Dair was talking about. He saw the other boy jump and then disappear below the roofline.

When Jake reached the place where Dair had disappeared, he saw the reason the other boy yelled. There was a massive chasm between the roofs. Jake slammed on the brakes and stopped right before going over the edge. Dair had made the jump and waited for him on the other side.

"Stop!"

Jake turned around and froze.

The monster guard from the vault was coming for him.

CHAPTER 8

Jake refused to panic. He backed up and made a running leap across the gap. His body slammed into the rocky roofline on the other side, but at least he was safe. Dair grabbed his arm and lifted him to his feet.

Jake never looked back. He didn't hear the giant anymore. Did the monster man not make the jump?

"Dair, I've got to take care of these," Jake said, holding up the money bags.

"Okay, but we have to move quickly. That guard in the vault—Vi—let us escape. Ka'nah will send more men to hunt us down. And trust me, we don't want to get caught."

Dair led Jake across a few more rooftops and down a handful of winding stone stairways until they had successfully escaped the compound. Jake saw the man whom he had taken the money from, sitting in the dirt in front of the same stone structure.

"Here's what I took, plus interest." Jake put both bags in front of the man. "Forgive me, but it helped me find my friend. Thank you."

The man yelled something Jake couldn't understand, but as he picked up both money bags, the anger in his voice faded.

Dair urged Jake to move.

Jake left the man to his money and took off after Dair. When they came to the city gate, Dair stopped.

"It's late, and you need rest. I'll keep watch while you sleep, and then you can do the same for me."

Jake looked around. They were in the wide-open entryway to the city. It was the same part of town where Jake had first seen his new friend. "Can we go to your house?"

"Not yet. That's the first place Ka'nah will check for us. We'll hide here in the open. You have to trust me. Get some rest, and we'll come up with a plan to rescue Levi."

Jake nodded. He sat down against the stone wall and tried closing his eyes. At some point sleep took over, and Jake let it.

ooooo

The next morning, after a little sleep and a long night of keeping watch while Dair slept, Jake opened his eyes and found Dair having a conversation with a group of boys who appeared to be teenagers. Another long trumpet blast rattled through the air. Jake looked around on the ground and grabbed a small stone to add to his collection of two. The Israelites were on their third march around the city of Jericho.

Four more to go.

"Jake, hopefully you are rested. These are my brothers Rehu, Jez, and Sebbi. They have offered to help us get Levi out."

Jake didn't understand why he was in this place. The only thing he had to hold on to was his sense of purpose. First, it was Dair. Then it was returning the blind man's money. Now it was the old man Levi who was on Jake's heart. He rubbed the stones in his pocket. He had no idea what was going to happen, but he trusted the Bible to be true. This whole city was going to be a gigantic pile of rubble soon.

"Let's go," Jake said.

Dair looked at him. "What's the plan?"

Jake put a hand on his friend's shoulder. "Come here." The two walked away from Dair's brothers to a section of the wall that provided a beautiful view of the plain. The morning sun rose strong and warm in the east, lighting up the land in brilliant shades of yellow.

"Dair, I want to be honest with you. I don't really have one. What I do know is that God's in charge, and I couldn't get you or Levi off my mind. So, just like I don't know why I'm here, I don't know how we will outwit Ka'nah, but I do know God will provide a way."

"No one gets off the ledge alive."

Jake didn't know where it came from, but he felt a sudden surge of boldness. "We will try."

Dair frowned. "Jake, you will be sent to the ledge for good. No turning back."

Jake had a thought from last year's social studies class. Harriet Tubman. After she had escaped, Harriet went back to the South and helped more people escape the bonds of slavery. It wasn't much, but if Jake could go back and get Levi out, it would feel like an accomplishment. "Dair, my God will go before us. We just need to trust."

"You are very odd, but I do feel there is something special about you. Let's get our plan worked out, and then we'll go for it."

Jake showed Dair how to high-five. "Amen."

Dair smiled. "You are strange, Jakehenry. But I like you."

ooooo

All five boys walked through Jericho, keeping their eyes peeled for any signs of Ka'nah's men. When they were almost back to the compound, Dair held up a hand.

"Hold on. I have an idea."

Jake was listening. "What?"

"There's something about you that I can't figure out, but I'm starting to believe what you say about your God and what you believe about this *Bible* story. If this place is really about to be destroyed, then let's help it along."

Jake stared at Dair, still not understanding what the other boy was thinking.

Dair continued. "Let's cause a massive distraction that will get Ka'nah's men out from the compound. Then we'll hurry in and grab Levi."

"Okay," Jake said. "Like what?"

"We're going to set the compound on fire."

Jake didn't want to hurt anybody. "How?"

"On the side where the ledge is, there are tons of storage rooms. Where Ka'nah keeps most of the things he steals. We will get in and set it on fire. Once the fire gets going, Ka'nah will pull Yod from the ledge and Vi from the vault to help put the flames out."

Jake still wasn't sure. "How are we going to start the

fire? His men will stop us."

Dair pointed to a corner of the compound that was closest to them. "We can go in from the outside. That little hole over there in the corner leads to the back side of the storeroom. Ka'nah leaves it open on purpose. He said it's just big enough for a man his size to squeeze through. It's an escape route if he ever needed to leave the compound unnoticed."

Dair explained that they had to wait until night to go in, so the boys stayed in the shadows, biding their time.

ooooo

When evening came and the sun set over the massive walls of Jericho, one of Dair's brothers headed for the hole in the compound wall. Jake and the others watched as Jez crossed a dirt path, got down on the ground, and crawled into the tiny opening that led into the compound.

"I told him to just check if anyone's in the room. If not, we will all go in and start the fire," Dair said.

A few minutes after Jez disappeared into the wall, he reappeared. A look of worry covered his face. "There are two men. I don't recognize either one of them."

"Okay, we will wait," Dair decided.

Hours passed as Jake and the others waited. At some point, he fell asleep and had a bizarre dream.

CHAPTER 9

His eyes couldn't make sense of anything. He had only an awareness of being in the middle of nowhere. Jake blinked, but the darkness remained. Even though he didn't know where he was or what was going on, he was overwhelmed with the urge to move.

He started walking and kept his hands out in front of his body in case there was something in his path. A light breeze ran across his face, carrying with it faint traces of salt water. It was like standing on a beach in the middle of the night with no moon or stars to light the way.

Jake's mind began creating scenarios that caused him to become afraid. Some crazy person was following him. The world was ending, and his last memory was only the darkness. This was what it felt like to die.

The ground had turned to water rushing around his legs. And it was rising. And so was the sun. The rays slowly erased the black world and let Jake know the source of the water.

Jake was standing in the middle of an ocean. The waves had risen up to his knees when the air started to move around him in angry rhythms, spinning the heavy water like it was blue cotton. Something, an unseen force, grabbed him and lifted him up out of the tempest and put him down on top of what looked like a massive wooden boat.

From this new vantage point, Jake could see a mountain of land rising up above the floodwaters. On the side of the great wall of earth, there seemed to be a crowd of people facing the water. Facing the crowd was a young boy who, to Jake, looked to be around his same age. Even though Jake was a good distance away, it looked like there were giants standing in the crowd.

Drops of water pelted his body as rain poured over the world in unrelenting sheets.

In the blink of an eye, Jake witnessed the side of the mountain collapse into the ocean, taking the boy with it. One of the giants threw something cylindrical down at the boy. Jake couldn't tell what it was but thought it was a part of a tree because the object floated after missing the boy and hitting the water. Jake watched the boy grab hold of the floating object and begin to move in Jake's direction.

A new wave of water crashed over the boy and knocked

him off what was surely a log.

The boat that Jake was on had started moving away from the boy.

Jake looked down and saw a man wrapped in a brown robe leaning out from a lower section of the boat. He stretched his arms out in the direction of the helpless boy. When he looked back out, the boy in the water had disappeared. Seconds later, Jake saw a glowing hand appear in the middle of the storm. It wasn't a human hand. Jake guessed the thing was at least the size of a two-story house, and it was radiating light.

The supernatural hand reached deep into the water and came back out in the shape of a fist. Jake watched the fist open to reveal the boy, who had tried in vain to battle the flood. It was like the owner of the supernatural hand wanted Jake to know that the boy had been saved.

ooooo

"Wake up!"

Jake opened his eyes. Dair was staring at him. "What?"

"We have to go. We think one of Ka'nah's men spotted us." As Jake stood, he heard the distant sound of the Israelites' trumpets. He bent down and grabbed a pebble from the ground. Number four. Only three to go.

Dair and his brothers led Jake to a part of the city

that was next to the ledge. They all looked and could see that Levi was still alive. Jake saw that the man's cloak had been torn apart in random swaths, from top to bottom. His face and arms seemed to be covered in scratches. The old man was hunched over instead of standing tall like the first time Jake had met him.

There was nothing to do but sit and wait until evening came.

And again, when night came over Jericho, the group went back to the compound and Jez crawled back through the hole. This time he was in a little longer before coming back out.

"Now there are three men in the room. Ka'nah has never had people in there. Maybe something's wrong."

"No, we're okay. We'll try again in a couple hours. If there's still men in there, then we will give it one more day. If nothing changes, we'll come up with a new plan," Dair said. Even though his brothers were older, it seemed he was the one born with an abundance of leadership skills.

The group stuck to the shadows again. This gave Jake a chance to think about his situation. What if he never made it back to camp? What if he never saw his parents again? Whatever happened, he knew God was faithful.

So Jake committed his time to praying that God's will would be done. On another note, Jake was excited that even at his young age, he was seen as worthy in God's eyes.

After the darkness of night grew deeper, Jez went back into the hole. And he again came out with a bad report. "This time there was only one guy in there, and while I was watching, he left. I thought we were good, but then he came back in and sat on the floor. He didn't seem to be in a hurry to leave."

Dair led Jake and the others away from the compound to find a place to get some sleep. They all took turns keeping watch. When it was Jake's turn to sleep, he had another crazy dream.

ooooo

The weight of another sleep brought him to another world. But this time, the darkness wasn't borne from the absence of light. This time, a huge desert sun was covered by a swarm of bugs—huge cricket-looking insects with white wings. The swarm kicked up a storm of sand, making it hard for Jake to see.

The light that did reach his eyes was a deep orange purple. Another mountain with hard lines and edges appeared on the horizon. It looked like a huge pyramid trying to peek through the wall of flying bugs.

Now Jake saw a girl standing at the base of the pyramid. She had on a white sleeveless shirt and jeans. He also saw she had a fabric bracelet around her right wrist. Like the boy in the ocean, this girl also looked to be about Jake's age. There had to have been millions of the bugs swirling around the girl, but she didn't seem to be affected by them.

Then the scene changed, and the same girl was now riding a horse. Jake's surroundings had changed too, and he was standing on the shore of what seemed like an endless sea. Another horse and another rider came into view, galloping hard, trying to catch up with the girl.

Jake turned and saw that the sea he had been standing next to was actually being split in two. Walls of water rose up, revealing a wide, dry path of earth. Jake saw tons of people walking right through the middle of the sea!

The girl had almost made it to the path that cut through the water when the man caught up to her. He shot out a hand and yanked her off her horse. The man stopped his horse and then got down to yank the girl to her feet. He slapped her. The earth groaned, and Jake felt like this was the craziest dream he had ever had. Surely this wasn't real.

The walls of water collapsed over the girl and the man. This had to be the story of the Israelites escaping from the

Egyptians through the Red Sea!

Jake was overwhelmed with saving the girl, so he ran. . .into the raging water. He tried swimming out to the girl, but the closer he got, the more hopeless his heart became. The water was too powerful. In fact, he was sure he could see the man's body being carried away on the unforgiving currents. The girl had to be gone.

But then Jake saw something that gave him the feeling he had been here before. The gigantic hand of light came down from the sky and plunged itself into the water.

Jake thought about the last time he had seen the hand. It had reached down and pulled a boy out of a raging ocean.

One thing was clear. This was a hand of salvation.

Now, here again, the glowing hand pulled out of the water and held up the girl who had only moments before gone under its unrelenting force. Then the hand took the girl away. . . .

ooooo

A trumpet blast pulled Jake from the wild dream. After he came to his senses, he counted the rocks in his pocket. Four. He looked around and picked up stone number five. In two more days this whole city would be destroyed. Jake really couldn't believe it.

The boys spent the day roaming the streets of Jericho,

trying to stay hidden and as inconspicuous as possible.

When night came, Jez went back through the hole in the compound wall. This time he came back with a favorable report.

"It's clear."

Dair stood tall. "Okay, here we go. There's a man who bakes bread three houses down the path. He has a fire burning all day long. He makes his awesome bread with the fire in the mornings, and uses the flames at night to forge steel. Next to the bread maker is a lady who sells cloth."

Jake took it all in and tried to guess Dair's plan. His new friend kept talking. "We are going to the baker and buying five pieces of kindling. We will then go to the cloth lady and buy five pieces of cloth. We will each wrap a piece of cloth around our wood to make a torch."

Rehu interrupted. "How are we going to light the torches and get through the hole in the wall?"

"Good question, brother. We won't light them until we get inside the compound. Ka'nah likes to have warm meals at a moment's notice. He has a kitchen fire burning all night long that is right next to the storeroom. We will quickly light our torches, run back to the storeroom, and set the plan in motion."

The group hurried and collected the supplies from the baker and the cloth seller. All five of them crawled through the hole and entered the empty storeroom. Dair went around a wall with his homemade torch and came back with the cloth on fire. "Hurry. The kitchen is empty."

Jake and the others lit their torches from the kitchen fire. They came back into the storeroom and set empty sacks on fire. The fire quickly spread across the wooden shelves. Jake couldn't believe what he was doing. But if this saved Levi, it would be worth it.

Jake felt the heat rise. It was amazing how fast fire moved. He hurried back out the hole, right behind Jez.

When they were all out safely, Dair led Jake and the others to a nearby roof so they could watch the result of their work.

"Jakehenry, thank you for coming here to help us hear about your God."

"You're welcome, Dair. I still can't believe I'm here." Jake watched the flames start to leap out of the hole they had just crawled out of. Men and boys were yelling and running out of the compound by the dozens.

Dair stood and pointed. "The whole east wall that runs from the storeroom to the ledge is wood. Ka'nah thought he was being crafty by making the ledge a place of punishment. He needed a door so he built the wall. All out of wood."

The boys sat there watching the compound burn. More yelling. More men and children pouring out of the compound gate.

"Dair," Jake said, "how will Levi get through the fire?"

"Good question, Jake. When I said we needed a diversion, I meant for him, not us. Levi and I talked many times that if one of us ever escaped the compound and the other had not, then the one who got out would come back and set a fire like we just did."

Dair remained silent for a minute. He watched the flames rise across the compound. "Jake, Levi means a lot to Ka'nah. I'm sure by now he has men going after Levi."

No sooner had he said the words than Dair's prediction came true.

Jake looked down at the compound gate and saw the huge Drax monster man walk out with Levi in his arms.

"He's taking him to a secret hideout. If we follow him, we might be able to save him." Dair's voice didn't sound so sure.

If it were possible, the night felt like it was getting

darker, and Jake had a feeling that the longer they waited the harder it would be to fight the big man. He was overwhelmed with the need to save Levi.

"I have to go," said Jake.

"Go do what?" asked Dair.

"Save Levi." Jake looked at the fire burning on the compound. "It has to be me."

Dair shook his head. "I'm sorry, but you saw the size of the guy holding Levi. We'd need an army of men to take him out."

"Dair, like I told you earlier, I have no idea how I got here or why I'm here." Jake's voice became stronger. "But the more I do here to help, the more I feel a part of something. I don't feel alone here. It's like God is using this to show me I'm never alone, and I always have a job to do no matter what I feel inside or how crazy the situation is on the outside."

Jake got up and went to the stairs. "Pray for me."

Dair looked at Jake like he didn't know what that meant.

Jake said, "That means talk to God. Ask Him to watch out for me."

Dair still looked confused. Jake didn't want Levi to get too far away. He said goodbye to his friends and went down the stairs from the roof to the ground. Then he jogged in the direction the huge man had gone.

ooooo

The only thing going in Jake's favor was that there weren't any side streets in this part of the city. This meant the giant who had Levi could only be on this main path. Unless he had gone into one of the doorways.

Then Jake saw them from a distance and ran quicker to catch up. He had no idea how a boy like himself would be able to go up against this monster of a man, but he was going to trust God for the results. As Jake closed the distance, he still didn't have any idea about what to do, so he yelled for the man to stop. When that didn't work, he ran in front of the man and waved his arms. That did work. The monster man stopped moving to consider Jake. Levi made eye contact with Jake and smiled.

"I need my friend," Jake said as he pointed at Levi.

The monster man laughed. "Get out of my way."

Jake still didn't have a plan. He stood his ground and asked a second time for the monster man to hand over Levi.

"You are in my way. Move before you get hurt."

Lord, please be with me!

"I came a really long way to get here. I'm not going

80

back without my friend."

The man put Levi down and took a huge step closer to Jake. Levi used the temporary freedom to run a safe distance away from danger, but close enough to keep an eye on Jake.

"You are foolish to think you can stand up to me." The huge man lunged at Jake and grabbed his arm. He swept Jake off his feet as fast as lightning. In seconds, Jake was hanging in the air, face-to-face with the giant.

Use what I've given you.

Jake felt the words in his mind. The only thing he had on him were the stones in his pocket. They weren't big enough to do much damage, but Jake had to have faith that it was enough. He grabbed them out of his pocket.

"I don't know who you are, but—"

Jake shoved the rocks deep into the man's mouth.

The giant tried to use his free hand to get them out, but he went into a choking fit instead. He couldn't squeeze the life out of Jake and choke at the same time. The need to survive won, and the giant let go of Jake.

Jake hit the ground hard. Pain shot up through his legs, but adrenaline helped him run. He made it to Levi. "Come on! The others are waiting!"

ooooo

When they got back to the roof where Dair and his brothers were waiting, Levi said, "Thank you, Jake. I didn't think I would ever see you boys again."

After they shared hugs, Dair said they should head out toward the main gate. If the city was going to collapse in a few hours it would be smart to get the rest of their family and get out. He quickly led Jake and the others through buildings and side paths until it was clear they were not being followed.

When night came, Jake spoke. "Thank you for believing in me. It feels good to be wanted."

Levi stood and spoke. "Jake, we are going to leave this place. I am so proud of you for having the courage to come here and rescue us."

Hours passed, and the group kept watch. The hours turned into a day and night, and when morning came, Jake heard the distinct trumpet blast pour up from the valley and down over Jericho. He looked and found six small stones to replace the five he used on the monster man plus the new one.

The morning hours turned into afternoon as the sun made its way across the Jericho sky. Waiting for tomorrow rattled Jake's nerves. What was it going to feel like?

An entire stone fortress city crumbling like a sand castle built too close to the water. And what if he was trapped in the debris?

Jake refused to think about it anymore. The truth was, he was going to rely on God. And God wouldn't let him down. No matter what things looked like, God was big enough to handle anything. When night came again, Jake was looking forward to seeing how it all was going to go.

Jake closed his eyes but had a hard time going to sleep. At some point, he thought about home. Would he ever go back? Would he be stuck here in this otherworld forever? After a long time of wondering about tomorrow, he fell into a light sleep.

ooooo

The next morning, Jake was exhausted. His only rest had been dotted with the bizarre dreams about kids experiencing Bible events and finding themselves in perilous situations only to be saved by some mysterious hand that came down from the sky.

He and Dair had slept on the roof, while the other three boys and Levi took turns keeping watch.

Rehu came up to Jake. "Our path is clear. But we need to leave now."

Jake let the excitement move him. Not being lonely and having a purpose was a great feeling. He was finally able to know what fitting in felt like.

But the feeling didn't last long. Ka'nah stepped out of the shadows and blocked Jake and the others from leaving.

"Hello, Jake. I don't want you to think you outwitted me. I let you take the old man and these boys. I needed to see whom I could trust. Obviously not these urchins." Ka'nah snapped his fingers, and five guards stepped up and grabbed Dair, Levi, and the other three boys.

"That leaves me and you. Should we play a game of kill the stranger?" Ka'nah closed the distance between him and Jake. His hand shot out and grabbed Jake's shirt before Jake could block him. "You and I are going for a walk."

CHAPTER 10

Jake was dragged all the way from the roof down through the alleys and streets of Jericho. Some people stared while others turned away. They were the ones who didn't challenge what was wrong with their world.

When they got to the doorway that led to the ledge, Ka'nah stopped and looked at Jake. "You don't belong here. I don't know how you got here, but I'm convinced that it's my job to make sure you never leave."

Jake was finally face-to-face with the end of his time in Jericho. The man who embodied evil and who lived to see other people suffer.

Ka'nah opened the door and pointed to the narrow precipice on the other side. "Head on out there." Ka'nah pushed Jake through the tiny opening. "You and your friends might have burned some of my compound, but as you can see it only ruined the storage room. The ledge is still beautifully intact."

The man spread his arms open wide.

Jake stopped himself on the small stone ledge.

"After you die, I'll have my men collect your body. I'll make sure you serve a purpose. You will be an example of what happens to people who try to cross me."

Jake stood on the rocky ledge and looked out over the valley far below. The last rays of sunlight painted the plain a deep purple. He sat down and let the situation soak in. He had tried hard, but it wasn't enough. He had come so close to helping Dair and the other boys escape Ka'nah's grasp. And here, on the edge of the world, Jake was right back where he had started. Alone.

As the sunlight faded and the darkness grew, night took over. Jake fell into a light sleep, but dreams still found him.

ooooo

This time it was different. Jake found himself standing on the side of a mountain looking down onto a vast plain. Above the plain was a city carved out of stone. It was broad daylight, and now Jake could see a massive throng of people who seemed to be marching. At the front of the procession, something was glowing.

The only darkness was a cloud of thick mist that hung

over the city. A figure stood on top of the city walls. The scene zoomed in, and Jake saw that it was his twin standing on top of Jericho. This was crazy, but it was so real.

The mist started to churn and cover the other Jake. Real Jake looked on from his hillside perch in shock. He was too far away to save himself, but he had to do something. The walls started to crack and fall. Huge slabs of stone began to peel away from the city and crumble down into the valley.

Jake watched his other self begin to run across the rooftops as the city literally fell apart behind him. Then he could run no farther. His other self was running one second, and swallowed up into the breaking earth the next.

Real Jake looked down and saw an army rush into the crumbling city with swords drawn. Soon, flames were licking the sky.

That's when Jake saw the glowing supernatural hand reach down from the heavens and scoop up a pile of debris. Some unseen wind blew all the unwanted rocks away and left only the other Jake sitting safe in the middle of the glowing hand. The hand lifted him up above the smoke and flames and continued to carry him a great distance away.

Real Jake felt like he was riding in an airplane watching all these things happen to the other Jake. He watched the hand descend through the clouds and come to a stop above *a chain of mountains. After a brief pause, the illuminated hand continued its descent over the mountaintops and farther down through the trees. It finally put him down next to a beautiful blue lake.*

At some point, the imaginary airplane landed, and Jake disembarked and found himself standing on the shore of a beautiful blue lake. It looked like the exact same one that he had seen from the plane. He had an urge to find the other Jake and ask him to explain what was happening.

When Jake turned around, the airplane was gone. He looked around and knew exactly where he was.

ooooo

The sound of trumpets pulled Jake from a deep sleep. Pieces of a bizarre dream clouded his vision. He turned and saw Ka'nah standing over him.

"Jake Henry," the wicked one said, "I can't believe I'm saying this, but I've had a change of heart. I want to give you credit for trying to not only save yourself but those four boys and Levi. I'm taking you off the ledge and bringing you into my inner circle. After all of your hard work trying to find a purpose here, I look at you and see that you're still all alone. Just like you started."

Jake counted the stones in his pocket.

Six.

The end was here. These trumpets were the last ones. Jake's brain tried to figure out a way to beat the evil man standing in front of him. But now it didn't matter, because if the Israelites were really on their seventh day of marching around the city, Jericho was about to fall. He remembered that they would march around seven times, so this was it. The end of all of it was finally here.

"Young Jake, I want to show you I'm not the evil man you think I am. I'm giving you one last chance to join me. You are very smart and brave. I don't want you to feel alone or left out."

A long blast of trumpets rang out. It was so loud, Jake thought the Israelites were just on the other side of the compound walls, not way down on the plain.

"No! I realize now that I am never alone! God is with me wherever I go."

Ka'nah pulled his sword from its sheath. He held the silver blade out toward Jake. "Well, I'm really sorry you believe that, because you are all alone whether you believe it or not. There's no one here to save you."

The shouts of thousands of men proved Ka'nah wrong. No sooner did the sound of voices end than the sound of the world breaking came over Jake and his enemy. The wall behind Ka'nah split in two like a piece of paper being torn in half. The ground shook, but Jake was able to keep his balance. Ka'nah, on the other hand, stumbled.

Jake jumped for the sword. The earth shifted again. Ka'nah regained his balance and yanked his blade away from Jake.

"God is here to save me!" Jake lifted both arms in the air, fists clenched.

Walls exploded and fell all around them. Off to his right, Jake saw the dorm building collapse like a sand castle punched by an ocean's wave.

Ka'nah ignored the destruction and swung the sword at Jake. Jake jumped back and missed getting cut in half by inches. He shook off the fear and refused to back down. Even though he didn't have a weapon, he was not going to go back to camp with regrets. If he ever got back to the camp.

Angry rocks shot past him in all directions, trying to rip his skin off his body as they flew. Groaning from somewhere deep within the ground beneath his feet threatened an even worse fate than being buried underneath the collapsing city.

Jake still couldn't believe all of this was really happening. He grabbed a chunk of stone and used it to block Ka'nah's next swing of the blade. Sparks flew as the sword connected with the stone. Another wave of earth-cracking energy ripped the ground under the compound. Jake fell down and saw that Ka'nah did too. The next thing Jake noticed was the sword wasn't in the wicked man's hand. It was on the ground halfway between them, lying across an opening in the ground like a narrow silver bridge.

Jake jumped and grabbed the sword before Ka'nah was able to stand to his feet.

The sword was very heavy, and Jake barely managed to raise it up to waist level.

"Please!" Ka'nah yelled over the groaning earth. "You're going to hurt yourself. Just give me the sword, and I'll let you go!"

Jake knew better. "No! You come and take it."

Ka'nah lunged at Jake.

Jake summoned all his strength and shoved the blade toward his opponent. The tip cut the man's right hand.

The ground shook and crumbled again. Jake fell down again but didn't let go of the sword. Rocks from a falling wall rained down over Ka'nah.

"Jake! Come on!" This was a new voice. A new sound in the middle of the chorus of collapsing walls.

Jake saw Dair standing on a pile of rubble on the far side of the compound. He yelled to Jake again. "Jake! You were right! The whole city is falling! Come on. Follow me!"

Jake went to where Ka'nah was being buried alive. He saw the man's hand reaching out. Jake bent down to see if he could help. It felt insane that one minute he was trying to protect himself from the madman, and the next he considered saving him.

"Come on, Jake! Don't worry about him! We're not going to make it if we don't leave right now!"

More groaning. More exploding rocks.

Jake let go of the idea that he would be the one to save Ka'nah. He took off running after Dair up over piles of fallen walls and crumpled homes. As he ran after Dair, Jake couldn't help but think what would happen if he died here. Would that mean he would also die in the real world back at camp? Or would it be like a dream where he would wake up right after the end came? Jake looked back and saw Ka'nah crawling out from under the rubble.

Dair was fast. The older boy moved like a mountain goat up and over the piles of Jericho that had collapsed all around them.

Jake looked back again and could not believe that Ka'nah had the strength to not only climb out from under the rubble, but also to use his long legs to catch up to his prey.

Jake's chest started to burn. He was running out of gas, but he couldn't quit now. He had come too far. He wasn't about to let the evil man catch him.

Jake concentrated and pumped his arms and legs as hard as they would go. Rocks shot across his path and rained down over him. Adrenaline surged through his veins and temporarily prevented him from feeling any pain.

"You are finished!" Ka'nah tackled Jake from behind. The force of the hit knocked the breath out of Jake's lungs. The wicked one got up and pinned Jake to the ground with one foot. He took his sword from Jake and swung it down.

Suddenly the earth screamed, and the ground fell away from him. Jake went flying backward. He watched Ka'nah's face let go of victory's grin in exchange for the frown of defeat.

The race had finally come to an end. Despite all his hard work and standing up to the very wicked man, the falling Jericho was seconds away from ending it all.

He had stood up bravely to the evil Ka'nah but didn't have the power to stand up against the forces of nature that were churning around him. As he flew down, Jake looked up and saw Ka'nah looking out over the chasm.

Jake crashed onto a pile of jagged stones. It was like diving backward into a concrete ocean. Stars of pain and light shot over the backs of his eyelids. Fire shot through his arms and legs. It felt like some invisible monster hand had squeezed his body and busted every bone. Twice.

The one who caused so much misery jumped and kept the sword out in front of his body. Ka'nah became like a bird of prey—a powerful falcon—zooming down to capture Jake. Jake was about to be pierced by the wicked man's sword, and he couldn't make his legs or arms work to get out of the way.

Where was Dair?

Muted voices came to Jake through the rubble. The sounds of men seeking their prey. Angry and determined tones got louder and clearer.

"Here's another one!"

Through the haze of his confusion from the fall, Jake was able to make out a mob of men holding weapons.

"Kill him!"

Ka'nah was right above Jake, blade extended, zooming

down for his own kill.

Jake shut his eyes and screamed.

Dair's voice came immediately to him. "He's with me!"

His body was yanked hard to the side.

He waited for the pain, but the piercing blow of the weapon never came.

A twisted clang and sickening crash echoed through Jake's ears.

Jake opened his eyes and saw that Dair was holding his arm.

The aftermath of Jericho falling reminded Jake of the war movies his dad watched. Mountains of rubble rose up around him. Dust hung in the air, making it hard to see and breathe. It was like the pieces of a giant stone puzzle had been dumped out all over the plain. . .all around Jake.

Ka'nah's body lay in a broken tangle inches away.

"I was there that day," Dair said to the men standing in a circle around Jake. "One of your men said we needed to tie a red ribbon in the window as a sign of the oath that our family would be spared."

The man lowered his sword. "Yes, that was our plan. I'm Joshua."

"Joshua! Yes, I'm Dair, brother of Rahab. These are

my brothers Rehu, Jez, and Sebbi. And our grandfather, Levi."

Jake couldn't believe any of this. Joshua? Rahab? And Dair was her brother? And Levi their grandfather? Out of all the people in this forsaken city, Jake had met Dair. Jake shook his head. God really was in control of all things.

"And who is he?" Joshua asked, pointing at Jake.

"He's with us. He's family." Dair smiled at Jake as he spoke the words.

It felt so good to be wanted.

CHAPTER 11

PRESENT DAY

NORTH CAROLINA

Jake opened his eyes and saw the glittering surface of the lake. The water rippled out in big bands toward the banks. Then he remembered skipping the rock out over the water before closing his eyes to take a quick nap in the grass. How long had he been out?

He looked at his watch. He still had thirty minutes before he had to be back to the cabin.

Déjà vu kicked in. Hard.

He had thought about taking that long walk in the woods, but now he remembered there was a man's deep voice that said—

Jake looked around to see if there was someone standing behind him.

But there wasn't anyone there. Just the trees.

And the path that led back up to the cabins.

Where did Jericho go?

As Jake turned back to look at the lake, it was still there. Beautiful water.

The camp had returned. The trees rose up around him just like the mighty walls of Jericho had done. Oak Bay had returned just as fast as it had vanished.

Definitely insane.

But everything wasn't the same. The lake and the trees were the same. The path back to the camp was the same. But something felt different. Jake couldn't put his finger on it, but something had definitely changed.

By the time he made it back up the path, huddles of boys had formed in front of the cabins. Jake walked over to his cabin and joined his cabin buddies.

"Hey, man. You just made it. Where did you go?"

Jake remembered feeling alone and unwanted. He remembered that none of the boys invited him to play and that's why he'd decided to go off on his own, down to the lake. And now, this kid had been watching. Had even noticed that Jake walked away on his own.

"The lake." Jake couldn't stop thinking about Jericho. "It was amazing!"

The boy gave Jake a look that suggested he thought the lake couldn't be all that exciting.

Jake just smiled.

The counselors materialized from their respective cabins and made their way to the center of the sea of boys.

One of them held a megaphone and used it to go over the cafeteria rules and behavior expectations. While he was talking, Jake noticed a new camper walking down the path. The boy was pulling a small silver suitcase and looked the same as Jake had felt walking down to the cabin for the first time. Except this kid was all alone. Most likely had said goodbye to his parents up in the main parking lot.

As the kid got closer, Jake saw he had a ribbon tied to the handle of the suitcase.

A red ribbon.

No way.

Jake felt compelled to introduce himself. He approached the boy and smiled.

"I'm Jake."

"Hi Jake. I'm Darius."

What? No way.

"What cabin?"

"Thirty-three."

Of course.

"Come on, that's my cabin too."

Jake showed Darius the cabin and told him about the lake. He was dying to tell him about the Jericho adventure, but he knew that would make him sound nuts.

"Jake, thanks for helping."

"No problem. I was supposed to be here with a friend of mine, but he got sick."

The other boy laughed. "No way. Me too. Good old Levi."

What?

"Levi?"

"Yes, my good friend, Levi Lewis. He invited me to come here with him. He came down with the flu or something, and here I am."

Jake was overwhelmed with anxious feelings.

What do I have to lose if I tell this guy about Jericho?

"Well, Darius, I sure am glad we're in the same cabin. Maybe this week won't be so bad after all."

Darius tossed his suitcase by the last empty bed and looked at Jake. "Yeah, I think so too."

They went back out and joined the group of boys who were already heading for the cafeteria. Jake's brain was exploding with memories of the Jericho experience. He decided that he would share it with Darius while they were eating.

"Jake?"

"Yeah?"

Darius stopped walking. He let the boys go into the cafeteria before he talked.

"Jake, I've been dying to ask you a question that's gonna sound bizarre, but I've got to ask it."

Jake felt his anxiety lessen a bit. "Sure."

"Did the guard at the gate seem weird to you?"

"Yeah! He stared at me as we drove in. A little psycho, if you ask me."

Darius stood there for a second, staring off into the woods.

Jake was on the verge of telling him about Jericho. What did he have to lose? Even if it freaked Darius out, what did it matter? It wasn't like he was ever going to see him again after camp ended.

"Yeah," Darius continued. "He stared at me too. But when my mom was asking him for directions to the cabin, the guy started talking about the Bible story of Jericho. My mom just kept nodding. Then she rolled up her window and drove off."

"Jericho?"

"You know, the place where the walls fell down. That Jericho."

Okay, that's it! I'm talking.

"Darius, can I tell you a story after we eat?"

"Sure. But why don't you tell me while we're eating?"

Jake thought about how the story would sound to the other boys who'd be sitting around them. "I think it needs to wait until we're done and by ourselves."

"Okay. Let's go hurry and eat so I can hear your story."

The boys joined the crowd of campers in the dining hall and went on to enjoy a completely unhealthy but righteous meal of pizza, mashed potatoes, and French fries. Jake had an ounce of self-discipline and added a spoonful of broccoli to the carbohydrate symphony.

After they finished dinner, Jake and Darius went out and stood on a big deck that overlooked the lake. The sun had gone down, and the sky lost its color. The boys stood in silence for a while, looking up at the sea of stars that glittered across the darkness.

Jake finally worked up the courage to tell his new buddy the whole story of his Jericho adventure. When he finished, he looked at Darius to see if he would be shaking his head.

"Jake, that is crazy."

I shouldn't have said anything.

"Yeah, you probably think I'm nuts. I don't know why I told you all that."

"Dude, don't worry about it. I'm so relieved."

"What?"

Jake watched Darius pull the red ribbon that had been on his suitcase out of his pocket. Jake hadn't seen him take it off the suitcase handle.

"Jake, something crazy is happening, because I have a story to tell *you*."

"Shoot."

"Okay, that guard back at the gate gave my mom two of these ribbons. He said one needed to go on my suitcase and the other was for a friend. I had no idea what that meant, but now I guess you're supposed to have this."

Jake took the ribbon. He had no idea what he was supposed to do with it. Tie it to his suitcase too? Surely not. He ran it through his fingers for a moment, trying to figure out what on earth was happening.

The guard at the gate.

Jake had to work up the courage to approach the guy, but at least he might get some answers. He told Darius his plan. "Do you want to come with me?"

"Sure."

Jake took a deep breath and put the red ribbon in his

pocket. "Okay, let's go."

The campground had an eerie feeling about it at night. There was no sun to light up the paths. Jake felt braver that Darius was with him.

It took a few minutes to reach the front of the camp, but when they saw the gatehouse, the boys stopped. Flames engulfed the tiny structure. There was no sign of the guard. Sirens wailed. Campers and counselors began to congregate in the parking lot to get a great view of the blaze.

"I guess we'll have to look for the guard tomorrow," Darius offered.

"Why wait for tomorrow?"

Jake and Darius turned in unison at the sound and found the guard standing next to them.

"What's going on?" Jake took the red ribbon out of his pocket and waved it in the guard's face.

The guard started walking to a cabin that wasn't far from the front gate. "Police are going with arson. Come on, I've got something I want to show you two."

Inside the cabin, Jake watched the guard's computer fire up and, after a few keystrokes, display a screen with

ELECTUS

The guard said, "Watch this." He hit a few more keys and then the word changed.

3L3CTUS

"*Electus* is a Latin word that means 'selected' or 'chosen.' And as you can see here"—the guard pointed to the reversed *E* at the beginning of the word—"both of these make the number—"

"Thirty-three," Jake interrupted.

"Exactly. That, my friends, is a very special number. But, lest I get ahead of myself, let me show you a few more things."

Jake and Darius stood behind the man and watched as he clicked on the word *ELECTUS*. The letters disappeared, and in their places was a list of titles that included *The Great Flood*, *The Ten Plagues*, and *The Fall of Jericho*.

"Jericho!"

"Are you familiar with that story?" the guard asked.

Jake nodded. He wasn't ready to tell everyone about his adventure, but he was familiar with the Bible story.

Jake watched as the guard clicked on *The Fall of Jericho*. The screen morphed into a picture of the walled city. It was the same exact view Jake had of Jericho when he first arrived there on the plain.

The cabin door opened. A young man with a camp T-shirt stepped in. "Hey, they need you."

The guard shrugged. "Coming." He turned to Jake and Darius. "I'll be right back. Wait here."

After he left, Jake was tempted to start clicking buttons on the guy's computer to get more information. He opted against it, not wanting to get into trouble.

Darius grabbed Jake's arm. "I think we should leave."

"Why? This is cool."

"Look." He pointed at a giant sword that was propped against the far wall.

Jake couldn't believe it. All the similarities. But he did agree with Darius. Something wasn't right about this guy. Both boys hurried out of the door and ran back to their cabin. Cabin 33.

○○○○○

The week flew by, much faster than Jake would have ever guessed it could. Now it was over, and he wasn't looking forward to going home. There were so many questions without answers. And he'd made a real friend.

As Jake followed Darius up the trail toward the main parking lot, he wondered about the future. Would he be able to experience any other Bible stories? Were there other kids like him who had their own adventures?

In his heart, Jake felt that God had somehow orchestrated the events of the past week to change their relationship. Before camp, Jake felt alone and unnecessary. Now, in some small way, he felt like he belonged.

"For the mountains may move and the hills disappear, but even then my faithful love for you will remain."

Jake finally knew the truth. No matter what might happen in life, he finally understood that God's love for him was as real as the trees that reached up around him. And God wouldn't be God if He gave love one day and took it away the next.

They made it to the parking lot and stood next to each other, looking for their parents. Darius was the first one to see his mother's car pull in.

"Okay, Jake. Let's keep in touch."

Jake gave his new friend a thumbs-up sign. "You bet!"

As he watched his new friend drive away, Jake was left to his own thoughts. God had been faithful. He loved Jake and had sent him Darius. Not to mention the whole Jericho experience. Feeling alone wasn't an option anymore.

"He's not going to keep in touch."

Jake was pulled out of his reflecting by the sound of a man's voice.

"You know that, right?"

Jake turned and saw that it was the guard. What was up with this guy?

"How do you know?"

"Dude. This isn't real. You're still not getting it, man. It's all part of the plan."

Jake started to walk away from the man. He had a weird feeling about him.

"Oh, Jake. You can walk away, but you can't hide from me."

Thank goodness, at the same moment, Jake saw his parents' car pull into the drive. When Jake turned to see if the guard was following him, all he saw were the other campers who were still waiting on rides. The guard had disappeared.

Jake waved at his parents, and they waved back. His dad parked the car and got out to greet Jake. His mom did the same.

"How was your week?" Jake's dad asked as he grabbed Jake's suitcase.

"Unreal."

Jake's mother gave him a bear hug. "I bet. We missed

you. Did you have a good time?"

"I met some new friends. Saw some amazing places. It was wild."

"I can't imagine."

I can.

The Henrys got back in the car and started out of the parking lot. Jake's dad pulled up to the burned-down gatehouse and stopped before pulling out onto the highway. The guard was there going through the rubble. He turned and waved at Jake's dad.

The guard's name tag said KEN NAH.

Unreal.

ABOUT THE AUTHOR

Matt Koceich is a husband, father, and public school teacher. Matt and his family live in Texas.

COLLECT THE SERIES!

Imagine... The Great Flood
The last thing ten-year-old Corey remembers (before the world as he knew it disappeared) was the searing pain in his head after falling while chasing his dog Molly into the woods. What happens next can't be explained as Corey wakes up and finds himself face-to-face with not one but *two* lions!

Paperback / 978-1-68322-129-6 / 112 pages / $5.99

Imagine... The Ten Plagues
Join the epic adventure of fourth-grader Kai Wells, who only remembers (before the world as she knew it disappeared) being surrounded by bullies on her walk home from school. What happens next can't be explained as she finds herself on the run for her life in ancient Egypt!

Paperback / 978-1-68322-380-1 / 112 pages / $5.99

Coming Soon!
Imagine... The Giant's Fall (releasing May 2019!)
The last thing fifth-grader Wren Evans remembers (before the world as she knew it disappeared) is getting off the school bus to discover her house engulfed in flames. What happens next can't be explained as Wren finds herself in a beautiful valley with a shepherd named David—in ancient Israel!

Paperback / 978-1-68322-944-5 / 112 pages / $5.99